This book belongs to:

_____

_____

_____

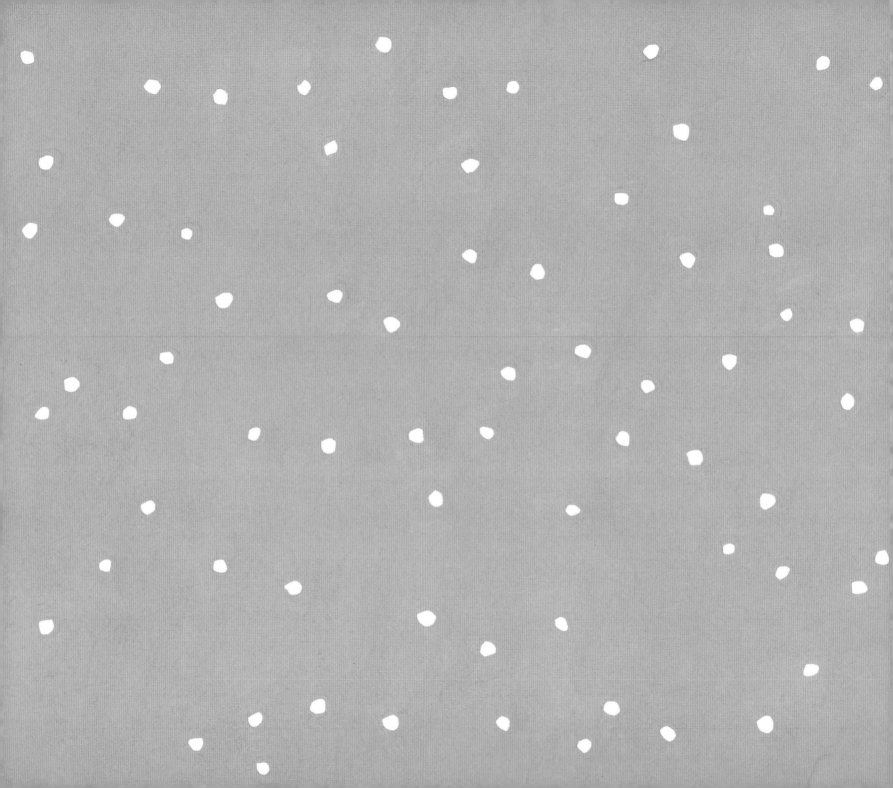

First published 2003 by Walker Books Ltd
87 Vauxhall Walk, London SE11 5HJ

This edition published 2012

2 4 6 8 10 9 7 5 3 1

The author/illustrator has asserted her moral rights
Illustrated in the style of Lucy Cousins by King Rollo Films Ltd
Maisy™. Maisy is a registered trademark of Walker Books Ltd, London

Printed in China

British Library Cataloguing in Publication Data:
a catalogue record for this book is
available from the British Library

ISBN 978-1-4063-4452-3

www.walker.co.uk

Maisy's Christmas Eve

Lucy Cousins

WALKER BOOKS
AND SUBSIDIARIES
LONDON • BOSTON • SYDNEY

Snow fell on
Christmas Eve.

Snow fell on
Maisy's house.

Snow fell on Charley's house.

Snow fell on Cyril's house.

Snow fell on Tallulah's house.

Snow fell on Eddie!

He was on his way to see Maisy.

Everyone was invited to Maisy's house for Christmas.

Flip-flap!

Cyril went on snowshoes and got there slowly.

Swoosh! Swoosh!

Charley and Tallulah went by sledge and got there quickly.

Plod-plop!
Eddie walked ...
and got stuck in
the snow!

At Maisy's house the snow fell thick and fast.
And it was ... COLD!
The friends hurried in to keep warm by the fireside.

Everyone got ready
for Christmas.

But where was Eddie?

They made mince pies, wrapped presents and put up paper chains.

But where was Eddie?

All together they decorated the Christmas tree.

But where was Eddie?

They all
went out
to look
for him.

They found a shed covered in snow.

But poor Eddie was stuck in the snow!

One, two, three ... PULL!
One, two, three ... PUSH!

Oh dear, Eddie was still stuck!

Then Maisy had an idea.
She fetched the tractor.

One, two, three ...

At last, Eddie was free.

That evening, everyone gathered around the tree to celebrate. Then the five friends sang Christmas carols together...

And Eddie sang
the loudest of all!

My friend Maisy

Maisy Goes to Bed

Lift the flaps! Pull the tabs!

A Maisy Classic Pop-up Book Lucy Cousins

ISBN 978-1-4063-0970-6

Maisy Goes Swimming

Lift the flaps! Pull the tabs!

A Maisy Classic Pop-up Book Lucy Cousins

ISBN 978-1-4063-0972-0

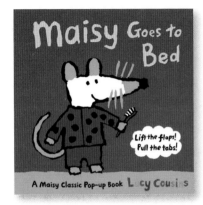

Maisy Goes to Playschool

Lift the flaps! Pull the tabs!

A Maisy Classic Pop-up Book Lucy Cousins

ISBN 978-1-4063-0971-3

Maisy Goes to the Playground

Lift the flaps! Pull the tabs!

A Maisy Classic Pop-up Book Lucy Cousins

ISBN 978-1-4063-0976-8

Maisy at the Farm

Lift the flaps! Pull the tabs!

A Maisy Classic Pop-up Book Lucy Cousins

ISBN 978-1-4063-0973-7

Maisy's ABC

Lift the flaps! Pull the tabs!

A Maisy Classic Pop-up Book Lucy Cousins

ISBN 978-1-4063-0974-4

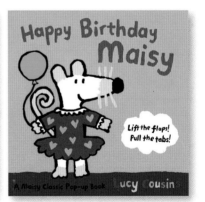

Happy Birthday Maisy

Lift the flaps! Pull the tabs!

A Maisy Classic Pop-up Book Lucy Cousins

ISBN 978-1-4063-0691-0

It's more fun with Maisy!

Available from all good booksellers

www.maisyfun.com